THE BEAR & THE FLY

a story by
PAULA WINTER

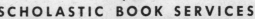

SCHOLASTIC BOOK SERVICES
NEW YORK · TORONTO · LONDON · AUCKLAND · SYDNEY · TOKYO

ISBN 0-590-31568-4

Copyright © 1976 by Paula Winter. All rights reserved. This edition is published by Scholastic Book Services, a Division of Scholastic Magazines, Inc., 50 West 44 Street, New York, N.Y. 10036, by arrangement with Crown Publishers, Inc.

12 11 10 9 8 7 6 5 4 3 2   0 1 2 3 4 5/8
Printed in the U.S.A.   07

For Norma Jean

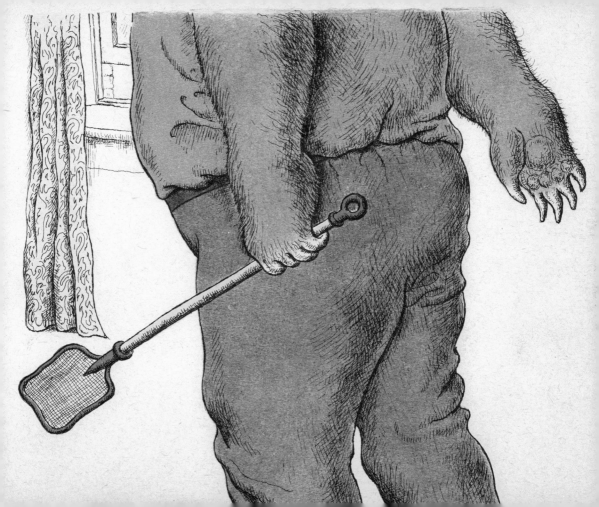